7|10

Especially for my Bakhtina

Also by David McKee

Elmer
Elmer and Rose

First American edition published in 2009 by
Andersen Press USA, an imprint of Andersen Press Ltd.
www.andersenpressusa.com

First published in Great Britain in 2009 by Andersen Press Ltd.
Published in Australia by Random House Australia Pty.

Distributed in the United States and Canada by
Lerner Publishing Group, Inc.
241 First Avenue North
Minneapolis, MN 55401 U.S.A.
www.lernerbooks.com

Library of Congress Cataloging-in-Publication Data Available.
ISBN: 978-0-7613-5154-2

Manufactured in Singapore.

2 - TWP - 10/23/2009

This book has been printed on acid-free paper.

ELMER'S
SPECIAL DAY

David McKee

Andersen Press USA

Elmer, the patchwork elephant, looked at the other elephants and smiled. It was almost Elmer's Day—the day when once a year all elephants decorate themselves and parade. The elephants had only just begun to prepare for it, but they were already excited and noisy.

"I say, Elmer," remarked Lion. "That's a bit of a racket your chaps are making!"

"I'm sorry," said Elmer, "but the preparations are as much fun as the parade itself."

"Only for elephants," said Tiger. "Be a good fellow and quiet them down."

"Please," said the monkeys.

A little later on, the other animals asked, "How about less noise from your friends, Elmer?"
"Please," said the rabbits.

Elmer went back to the
elephants. "The neighbors are complaining
about the noise," he said. "Let's be a bit quieter."
"Of course, Elmer." "Sorry, Elmer." "Certainly, Elmer."
"Right, Elmer." "Don't worry, Elmer." "We'll be
quieter than quiet, Elmer," the elephants promised.

But ten minutes later, the elephants were noisier than ever!
"Listen," said Elmer, "I've got an idea."
"Whatever you like, Elmer," said the elephants, as they
continued their preparations. "It's your Day!"

Elmer returned to the other animals.
"I'm sorry about the noise," he said. "But this year is a special year, because you are all invited to join the parade. Of course, you will have to decorate yourselves."
The animals were really excited.

Gradually every corner of the jungle became filled with the sound of laughter and preparations for the parade. "What a racket!" thought Elmer, looking at the elephants. "And what a mess! I wonder how the others are doing?"

The other animals were just as messy
and noisy as the elephants. Elmer chuckled. "Well
at least no one is complaining now," he thought.
"Do you mind, Elmer," said Bird. "We'd rather you didn't
spy on our preparations!"

At last the big day came. The tradition was that on Elmer's Day only Elmer could be elephant-colored. So as usual, Elmer went to the bush with the elephant-colored berries and covered himself with berry juice until he looked just like an ordinary elephant. Then he returned to the herd.

The other elephants were ready and waiting.
"The parade can begin as soon as the other animals
arrive," said Elmer. "Listen! Here they come!"

The elephants stared in amazement as the animals arrived.

Not only were the animals decorated, but they all wore elephant masks.

"You see, it's still an elephant parade!" Lion laughed.

"Let's begin," called Elmer from the front of the parade. "From now on everyone can join in the Elmer's Day Parade . . .

. . . as long as they wear an elephant mask!
This will be the best elephant parade ever!"

"And everyone," said Elmer, "means everyone!"